DALMATIANS

Cruella Returns

Adapted by
Justine Korman

Based on the teleplays "You Slipped a Disc" by Mirith
J. S. Colao, "The Cone" by Steve Granite and Cydne
Clarke, and "Snow Bounders" by Ken Koonce and
Michael Merton.

DISNEY
PRESS

New York

Printed in Mexico.

The text for this book is set in 16-point Berkeley Old Style.

ISBN: 0-7868-4134-6

Contents

1 An Unlucky Day. 1

2 A Slipped Disc 6

3 Enemy Territory 13

4 Into Orbit 20

5 Cone Alone 27

6 There's No Fun Like Snow Fun! . . . 35

7 Blame It on the Blizzard 45

8 The Best Place in the World 51

Chapter One

An Unlucky Day

My name is Lucky—too bad I don't feel lucky today. It's been one of those anything-that-can-go-wrong-will-go-wrong days. And it's all because of Cruella De Vil.

Woof! She makes me so mad!

With Cruella and me, it was hate at first sight. As soon as we met, Cruella dognapped me and my littermates.

1

But Cruella didn't count on the bravest dogs since Thunderbolt, P.I.—my dad, Pongo, and my mom, Perdy. Yeah, we showed Cruella who was top dog! But Cruella never quits. You'd think she'd get tired of chasing our tails.

It all started this morning in Roger's studio. Roger has the coolest job. He invents video games.

None of us pups are supposed to go in Roger's studio, because of the computer, the toys-that-aren't-for-chewing, and all this weird old stuff that people like to have around for no good reason.

I sneaked into the studio anyway. Roger was there and he was so happy! He was tippy-tapping on his computer keyboard. I could tell Roger was really excited.

"This is good!" Roger barked.

"This is *very* good!" he crowed.

I sneaked around behind Roger, trying to see his computer screen.

"My best work yet!" Roger exclaimed.

I just had to see what he was doing.

"I've outdone myself!" Roger cried. If he'd had a tail, he would have been wagging it.

I tip-pawed closer. I was almost there when Roger suddenly took his eyes off the screen and spotted me.

"No, no, no, Lucky," he said, scooping me up into his lap. "I know you're curious, but this is top secret."

3

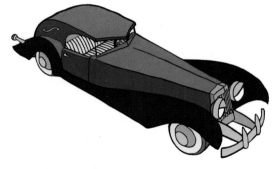

Just then, we heard a loud engine. I gritted my teeth at the familiar sound of Cruella's car.

Ker-rash, squeeeeeeal! Cruella crashed right into the birdbath.

Roger jumped out of his chair and looked out the window. Then he glanced back at the computer and me. Roger said, "No one must ever see this—especially not her."

Suddenly, he sprang into action. Roger popped the disc out of his computer and put it in an envelope. Then he licked the envelope, stuffed it in a sock, dropped the sock in a shoe, laced up the shoe, shoved it in a shoe box, pushed the shoe box under his desk— and put me on top of the shoe box!

Roger looked me in the eye and said, "Lucky, don't let anything happen to this disc. Guard it with your life. Got it?"

My chest puffed with pride. I gave a deep bark that meant, "You can count on me!" But as soon as Roger went downstairs to deal with our obnoxious, birdbath-wrecking neighbor, I just had to sneak a peek!

I opened the box, untied the shoe, pulled out the sock—you get the idea. Then I  popped the disc in the computer and . . .

A scary villain voice said, "The Cruellanator!"

Chapter Two

A Slipped Disc

The screen lit with a picture of my least favorite person in the world: Cruella De Vil! An announcer's voice reeled off the Cruellanator's vital statistics:

Age: 950
Brain: Tiny
Feet: Big
Breath: Bad
Hair: Bulletproof

Roger was right! This was great stuff! He had Cruella down pat. There was even this cloud of green coming out of her mouth. I could practically smell Cruella's bad breath.

And when the announcer got to the "Bulletproof" part, all these bullets zinged and pinged off Cruella's crazy, two-tone hair. (Have I mentioned the hair yet? This woman's hair is black, white, and ugly all over!)

I glanced back at the door and listened for footsteps, but the coast was clear. My tail was thumping with excitement as the announcer continued:

Your mission: Take. Her. Out.

The Cruellanator robot dissolved in the coolest explosion ever! I thought my tail would out-thump itself. I had to tell the gang—or burst!

"Rolly! Cadpig!" I barked. No one

answered. Typical! Rolly and Cadpig are always tagging after me—except when I need them.

When I turned back to the computer, there was Scorch! Scorch is a ferret, which is like a weasel—only worse! Scorch is also Cruella's pet. Need I say more?

In a blink, the sneaky little fur snake had grabbed Roger's disc! I lunged for him, but you wouldn't believe how fast that ferret can slink.

We totally trashed Roger's desk. Rolodex cards went flying everywhere like a paper blizzard. I practically got buried under a huge stack of books.

I chased Scorch and stopped him at the door. Then, suddenly, Scorch was out the skylight and onto the roof—with Roger's disc!

I raced downstairs and slammed right

into Cadpig. Ouch! She and Rolly were in the driveway trying to figure out what the busted birdbath was doing there.

Rolly just stood there, blinking at me.

"Rolly, you gotta help me!" I could barely get out the words.

But did I get support from my brother, my littermate, my pal? Rolly said, "Don't tell me. I don't want to know."

I told him anyway. "Scorch stole a disc and we gotta get it back or I—I mean, Roger—will be in big trouble." Even if Rolly wouldn't get off his large bottom for me, I thought he might do it for our pet's sake.

Rolly shook his head and walked away.

"Wow, sounds like a lot of work. Good luck with that. See you later."

Can you believe I call this guy my friend? I just don't get Rolly sometimes. "Come on! We can still catch Scorch before he gets to Cruella!"

Cadpig squealed. "Ooh! The thrill of the chase!"

None of us can ever resist the call to adventure. Maybe it comes with the spots.

In a flash, we were up and running. "This way!" I barked. "I know a shortcut!"

Thanks to my great leadership, we were

at Villa De Vil just in time to see Scorch slide through his ferret door into the mansion.

Even if Cruella hadn't pupnapped us for that crazy coat scheme, I'd have to hate her for her taste alone. And this morning the view of her hideous mansion was especially ugly, because we could see Cruella in a top-floor window. She actually manages to be ugly long-distance. As Cadpig would say, "That's a talent."

"Gee, I'd love to help you get the disc," Rolly began. "But I think—"

"There's no time to think!" I barked. "We have to act *now!*" I couldn't let Cruella get that disc. It might ruin everything. We might even lose the farm! Rolly and Cadpig had to

11

understand the importance of our mission.

I tilted my head back and said, "Let's do it for Roger!"

Cadpig caught the spirit right away. "Let's do it for Roger!" she cried.

Even Rolly managed to sound like a brave musketeer when he added, "Let's do it before dinner!"

Chapter Three

Enemy Territory

We squeezed through the ferret door into the ugliest
house ever built. Each wall is
covered in a different wall-
paper that clashes with
everything else. But worst of
all, every place you look
there's a portrait of Cruella
De Vil.

Suddenly Cadpig barked,
"There's Scorch!"

I looked up just in time to see the ferret making for the big double staircase. "He's going straight for Cruella!" I cried.

I tore up the left side of the staircase; Cadpig covered the right. Rolly wasn't about to exert himself, so he stayed on the ground floor while Cadpig and I chased Scorch.

I pounced but ended up with a face full of ugly carpet. Then Cadpig cornered him. "Freeze, ferret!" she commanded.

But Scorch snarled—then jumped right over Cadpig! I told you he was sneaky.

We chased that nasty ferret all over Villa De Vil. The minute we'd get the disc, Scorch would grab it back. That ferret's so slippery, I'd swear he's part eel.

Finally, Scorch managed to get all the way up to Cruella's study. I couldn't believe it!

14

There she was sitting at her computer—
and there was Scorch holding the disc!

Scorch jumped up and down, trying to
get Cruella to notice him. But Cruella was so
caught up in herself she didn't see anything.

But she couldn't miss it when the disc
went flying up in the air, hit the ceiling fan,
and landed—*click*—right in her computer
drive. Scorch and I dove for it and—

Ka-chunk! The disc fell into place.
Cruella's computer whirred to life, and I
heard the announcer's voice shout:

"The Cruellanator!"

That's when I decided I'd finally had enough
of my neighbor,
Cruella De Vil.

"Come on, guys!"

I raced out of the study and found Cadpig and Rolly cowering in the hall. "Let's get out of here!" I barked.

But they were a bit surprised when I didn't head for home.

"Is this another shortcut?" Rolly wondered. "I hate shortcuts."

I shook my head. This was not going to be easy to explain. "No, it's not a shortcut."

Cadpig had to trot to keep up with me. "So, are we going home by way of the North Pole, or what?" she panted. "'Cause if we are, I'd like to visit the—"

I wasn't in the mood for Cadpig's sarcasm. "We're running away, okay?!" I shouted. Sometimes it's hard to keep your cool.

"What?!" Rolly exclaimed.

"Running away. At least I am. You can

16

come if you want," I said. Actually, I hadn't even made up my mind until Cadpig started in with that North Pole stuff. But really, it's more than a dog can take to live next door to that . . . Cruellanator!

"I see," Cadpig said.

I hate it when she says that.

"*We're* running away because *you* let Roger down, and you don't want to go home and face the music," Cadpig continued.

I wasn't about to listen to her. "Are you with me or are you going to put up with Cruella De Vil for the rest of your life?" I said. Things were suddenly very clear. "Do you realize she's behind every bad thing that's ever happened to us?"

Rolly looked thoughtful. Even Cadpig was listening. I was on a roll. "Remember the time

I had stitches in my paw?"
I asked.

Cadpig giggled. "Who
can forget that way-cool
cone you had to wear around your neck?"

Rolly laughed, too. "You looked like a clown!"

"Thanks a lot, guys. But think back:
wasn't it all Cruella's fault?" I persisted.

Cadpig looked blank.

"Remember, she wasn't exactly invited to
that picnic. She just showed up," I said.

Rolly nodded. "Typical Cruella."

"That's what we're running away from!" I
exclaimed.

Cadpig still looked skeptical.

"Well, if she hadn't barged in on our picnic,
I never would have run into her," I explained.

"You're always running into everyone

because you never look where you're going," Cadpig said.

"You're just mad from this morning, when I ran into you in the driveway," I said. "But my point is, Cruella shouldn't have been at that picnic. And she was the cause of all the trouble that followed. Don't you remember? We were playing Frisbee in the field . . ."

Chapter Four

Into Orbit

My cone troubles began at a family picnic. I was in a bad mood. Three throws in a row, Mooch had grabbed the Frisbee. Mooch and his gang of bad pooches sort of came with the place when the Dearlys bought it.

Anyway, Mooch was hogging all the fun, as usual. And just because he's bigger than I am, he acts like he has the right. But I wasn't about to let him get away with that. So on the next toss, we both caught the Frisbee at the same time.

I wrestled and snarled with all my might. And suddenly, he let go of his end! I went flying through the air as if *I* were a Frisbee.

Flying would have been cool, except this was no amusement-park ride. Almost as soon as I was up, I started to come down!

There wasn't time to look where I was going, much less do anything about it. So I wound up colliding with Cruella, who was standing on the edge of Hiccup Hole. We both went tumbling into the pond.

An unexpected bath with Cruella was the least of my troubles. My airborne adventure left me with a big cut on my paw. Dr. Winokur, our vet, had to put in a few stitches. But that wasn't the worst of it. I had to wear a stupid plastic cone around my head so that I couldn't pull out the stitches.

And even *that* wasn't the worst of it. Cruella sprained her ankle and decided to milk this injury thing for all she could. She stayed at the Dearly farmhouse, with her feet up, ordering Anita and Roger around like servants.

Meanwhile, thanks to the cone, I was the laughingstock of the farm. Even the chickens were laughing at me. And I don't mean my friend Spot. I'm talking about the chickens who are such chickens they *never* cross the road.

My friends tried to help by wrapping

the cone in this huge woolen scarf. Spot squawked, "Perfect! The ascot makes you look positively distinguished!"

Rolly chimed in. "You look like a defensive tackle with a sore throat."

I said, "Oh, that's cool—*not!*"

"Now don't be a gloomy Gus," Cadpig cooed. "Come on. Let's try it out."

I was dying to know if it would work, too, so I stepped out of the barn into the sunlight. All the animals were out in the yard enjoying the nice day.

The cows were chewing, because that's about all cows do, really. The pigs were wallowing in the mud. The chickens were scratching. The other Dalmatians were playing. And I was out there with them in my cone—and nobody was laughing.

"Wow! This is going great!" I said.

So naturally, that's when everything went wrong. Mooch and his gang showed up. Mooch said, "Hey, look, guys. It's an outboard puppy. Let's rev him up!" Then he grabbed one end of my scarf and yanked.

Suddenly, I was spinning like a top! And once again, thanks to that mean mutt, I was in orbit!

I went flying through the kitchen door and landed on the tea cart. All the dishes clattered and the wheels started rolling, and the next thing I knew I was cruising through the family room headed straight for . . .

Cruella De Vil.

The cart was going so fast by the time it hit Cruella that we both smashed into the wall and knocked over a whole bunch of those toys-that-aren't-for-chewing. They break way too easily, if you ask me. The weird thing is, I'm positive I had seen Cruella on her feet heading for a box of chocolates just before we crashed.

Cruella had the nerve to blame the whole thing on me! She even told Roger, "I demand that the beast be locked up forever!"

What a creep! At least Roger stood up for me. He held me in his arms and said, "Sorry, Cruella. That's just *not* going to happen."

Cruella shrieked, "Fine. Have it your way, Rupert."

She never calls Roger by his right name.

"I *was* just going to sue you for the farm. But now I'm taking everything you've got!" Cruella continued.

I was scared. Roger was, too. I could feel it. Poor Anita looked like a deer caught in the headlights. What were we going to do?

Chapter Five

Cone Alone

Well, for one thing, I was
going to get out of that stupid cone! How could I help
Roger with that thing on?

Rolly, Cadpig, and Spot agreed to help
me get the scissors, which were in the sewing
basket on the top shelf of the closet.
Unfortunately, the only way we could reach
the basket was by climbing on top of each
other's shoulders. I was on the bottom, with
Rolly on top.

"I think I see it," Rolly said. "But this big round heavy thing is in the way."

"Heavy" doesn't begin to describe what Rolly took out of the closet. It was a bowling ball! We nearly fell over from the weight. And that was when Cruella rolled up in her wheelchair.

Cruella whipped out her portable tape recorder and said, "Memo to myself: Tell my doctor I'm not paying him *real* money for bandaging *fake* injuries."

Wow! I was so surprised I forgot all about trying not to fall and . . . we fell! The bowling ball went flying out of Rolly's paws—and landed right in Cruella's lap. Her wheelchair zoomed backward, through the open cellar door, and *bump-bump-bump-crash* down the stairs!

Cruella had been faking everything else. But that little trip to the basement really had to hurt!

By that afternoon, she was installed in an upstairs bedroom of the Dearly farmhouse, wrapped in more bandages than a mummy. She was planning to make Roger and Anita miserable for the rest of their lives.

But I had the solution! I just had to convince the others to help me. Sometimes it isn't easy being the one with the plan. All Cadpig could think about was my stupid cone. She wanted to paint black spots on it to make it blend in.

While Cadpig painted, I explained things to Spot. "We need to get Cruella's tape recorder. You heard her. She's faking this whole thing!"

 Cadpig put down her paintbrush to admire her work. "There! Practically invisible."

I didn't care if I looked stupid. I had a mission—to get that tape.

Cadpig, Rolly, Spot, and I sneaked up to the bedroom where Cruella was staying. Anita was spoon-feeding Cruella.

(Actually, full-body bandages look good on Cruella. With her, the less you see the better.)

Anyway, we crawled under the rug and wriggled across the room to her bed. Spot spotted the tape recorder on the nightstand near the tray of food.

I reached up and edged the recorder off the table. I caught it just before it hit the floor. It was so cool!

I whispered to the others, "Got it! Let's get out of here."

We were almost at the door when Cadpig said, "Hey, where's Rolly?"

I knew the answer even before I looked back. The food tray! Sure enough, there he was at the nightstand, reaching for the donut on Cruella's tray.

"Rolly! Come on!" I whispered as loudly as I dared.

How could he think of food at a time like that? But, hey, this was Rolly. He *always* thinks of food.

"Just one donut!" Rolly begged.

My stomach lurched. When you've been in trouble as often

as I have, you get so you can feel it coming.

Spot tried to pull Rolly away, but Rolly wouldn't give up. And suddenly, the tray went flying! Hot chili, mashed potatoes, and donuts rained down on Cruella De Vil.

Cruella screamed! She moved her arms and legs so fast they got all tangled up in their traction wires.

The whole thing collapsed in a mess of wires, bedsprings, and slippery chili. I wound up airborne—again!

This time I landed hard on top of Cruella's chest. By the time the dust cleared, the recorder was in my mouth and the spotted cone was around Cruella's neck!

Cruella got so mad, she burst right out of her cast and started chasing me all over the house!

"Give me that!" Cruella cried as she flung herself at me. She grabbed my neck, and the tape recorder went sailing out of my mouth. It landed on the floor and clicked to life. Cruella's recorded voice filled the room:

"*Tell my doctor I'm not paying him real money for bandaging fake injuries.*"

Roger grinned. "Fake injuries? My, my!"

Anita pulled me free of Cruella's clutches.

But I wasn't free of the cone just yet. In fact, Dr. Winokur gave me an even bigger one to wear—for the next month!

Of course, I wasn't the only one wearing a stupid plastic cone. House of De Vil dazzled the fashion world that season with *la Cone*!

33

No kidding! Cruella actually convinced all these rich humans to wear plastic cones around their necks in the name of looking cool. Even the other puppies on the farm wanted cones. Guess I was born to be a trendsetter.

Chapter Six

There's No Fun Like Snow Fun!

Cadpig's giggle brought me back to the present. "Remember how Two-Tone, Dumpling, and Dipstick all wanted a cone like yours, once Cruella made them fashionable?"

Rolly laughed. "You have to admit that was pretty funny."

I couldn't believe what I was hearing. "Are you

35

trying to tell me you think Cruella is funny?"

Cadpig snorted. "About as funny as a toothache. But—"

"But nothing!" I barked. "Are you forgetting that time we went snow camping?"

Cadpig shivered. "I'm not senile!"

Rolly shuddered. "I get cold and hungry just thinking about it."

"You're always hungry," I said. "My point is, we would have had a great time that weekend—if not for our neighbor, Cruella De Vil!"

Cadpig looked skeptical. "Um, wasn't it *your* idea for us to stow away in Roger's luggage?"

"Well . . . we couldn't let Dad and Roger be all alone for a whole weekend of fun, could we? Besides, how else would they realize we were ready to go camping?"

"As I recall, Dad realized we were ready

to be grounded for a week," Cadpig replied.

I hate it when she gets like that! "Okay, okay, so it was my idea to stow away. But who told Cruella to be on the same mountain? I mean, why does she always have to be wherever we are—just in time to ruin everything?"

Rolly nodded. "That *would* have been a great sled ride—if we hadn't run into Cruella."

The conditions were perfect! Mount Grutely Park sparkled with snow. Pine trees scented the crisp air.

While Dad and Roger made camp, Rolly, Cadpig, Spot, and I sneaked out of Roger's duffel bag and into the woods. We climbed a steep hill. At the top, I spotted an old yellow road sign lying on the ground just begging to be turned into the coolest sled ever!

Rolly and Cadpig jumped on right away. Spot was . . . chicken, at first. Considering what happened, I don't know if she was chicken so much as, well, right. But anyway, it looked like fun at the time, so I gave the sign a push and leaped on as it started to pick up speed.

And, boy, did it ever pick up speed. We were flying!

And then suddenly . . . *Cruella!* We smashed right into her! All of us went tumbling down a steep gorge.

Every inch was full of danger: a tree branch here, a half-hidden root there. We tried to steer, but everything was happening too fast.

On one of the bumps, Cadpig lost her

hold on the sign. Spot and Rolly fell off next. Finally, I couldn't hang on any longer.

While Cruella cruised down the hill on my sled, I rolled down in a growing snowball. The others were turning into living snowballs, too!

At the bottom of the hill, we all rolled on top of Cruella.

"Photo-shoot saboteurs!" she shrieked.

We found out later that Cruella had come to the park to take pictures of her new line of camping gear. You can bet she wasn't there to appreciate nature.

We tried to get away from Cruella, but the hill was too steep. And this may sound really strange, but we were . . . worried about her. Suddenly poor taste, bad breath, and even the fact that she was Cruella De Vil didn't matter anymore. She was just a person who'd hurt herself.

Fortunately, Cruella had an amazing inflatable tent with her. Unfortunately, she passed out trying to blow it up. We blew it up for her, hoping that she'd let us share. No chance!

Then Cruella shot off a flare. Spot, Cadpig, Rolly, and I all hoped it would bring Dad and Roger to rescue us. But everything went wrong, as usual. The flare sailed up into the air—and came back down, right on top of the tent.

Cruella wailed, "Noooooo!"

In seconds, it was a puddle of molten rubber. Cruella pulled out her mini tape recorder and grumbled, "Memo to myself: next time, include inflatable fireman!"

The recorder made a weird squealing

sound. Cruella shook it, then cried, "This doesn't work, either? *Arghh!*"

She tossed the recorder over her shoulder. It landed at the base of a QUIET, AVALANCHE DANGER sign. The switch clicked against the sign post, and the recorder played back Cruella's yell at top volume: *"Arghh!"*

It echoed all over Mount Grutely Park. The echo turned into a thundering rumble that shook the ground.

Luckily, the avalanche only buried Cruella. Unluckily, she didn't stay down!

By then we were getting awfully cold. And it was starting to snow!

"I've got to find shelter. But how will I get there?" Cruella wondered.

Then she spotted us and the sign we rode in on. The next thing we knew, Cruella had

41

us hitched up to the sign like sled dogs.

Cruella snapped the ropes like reins. "Mush, you mutts!" she commanded.

And for some reason, we did! I guess you'd call it the survival instinct. We pulled as hard as we could against that freezing wind.

Then Cruella suddenly exclaimed, "Salvation!"

I wiped the snow from my eyes. Then I saw the cave, too.

We followed Cruella inside. She found a hibernating bear!

Cruella kicked him awake. "Scram, Smokey. Break time's over!"

The bear growled. Cruella growled back at him! The bear gave a frightened whimper and ran off.

While she curled up on the bear's bed of leaves, we tiptoed closer. Just being out of the bitter wind was a big relief.

"If only I had a fire, this place wouldn't be too abysmal," Cruella observed.

She looked down at her hideous House of De Vil poncho. Cruella pulled it off and rolled it in a ball. Then she patted her pockets.

"Where's my lighter?" Cruella muttered. Then she gasped. "In my purse! Where's my purse?"

I knew where it was. "She dropped it back where we fell. Let's go get it."

I was convinced that if we helped Cruella she would help us. I guess it was that survival thing.

Spot thought I was crazy. "Go back there

through this gizzard-freezing blizzard?"

"We've got to work together to get through this," I said. Things were serious. Even Cadpig could see that.

"Lucky's right," she said. "Survive now, blame Lucky later."

As we left the cave, I heard Cruella snap her cane in half and mutter, "Fortunately, I'm part Algonquin."

I thought, Lady, you are part gargoyle! But there was no time to waste on insults.

While Cruella rubbed her sticks together, Rolly, Cadpig, Spot, and I walked back out into that terrible storm.

Chapter Seven

Blame It on the Blizzard

 By then the snow was so high we could barely walk. Rolly held my tail in his mouth. Spot held Rolly's. And Cadpig held Spot's tail feathers.

For a moment I thought, We're not going to make it! I pictured Dad and Roger finding our frozen bodies. I imagined Dad howling with grief and saying, "I knew they weren't ready for camping!"

Somehow that made me mad enough to go on.

Finally, we reached the base of the gorge where we'd all landed in a heap. I spotted Cruella's purse strap poking out of the snow. I grabbed it and pulled the purse free.

Then we trudged all the way back to the cave. Everything was numb by the time we got there. Instead of paws I seemed to have lead weights.

Cruella was still crouched over her sticks. She'd rubbed them down to toothpicks but still hadn't gotten a spark.

When Cruella spotted her purse dangling from between my chattering teeth she squeaked "Give me that, you purse snatcher!"

I could hardly believe my numb ears. We risked our lives—and froze our tails—to get

 that hunk of junk, and . . .

Cruella snatched the purse and pulled out her lighter. Click . . . *whoosh*! Suddenly, a giant flame leaped out and ignited the poncho. Cruella stretched out her bony fingers to the flame.

My heart sank. I was cold, hungry, and scared. We'd tried everything I could think of, even helping our creepy neighbor. And it hadn't worked!

Then something amazing happened. Cruella looked at the four piles of spotted snow shivering in front of her and said, "Oh, all right. But stay on your side of the fire. I don't want you absorbing any heat from my side."

She didn't have to ask us twice. We scrambled close to the flames. It felt so good!

But, of course, the poncho couldn't burn forever. By the time it was ashes, Cruella was fast asleep—and we were freezing again.

I knew what we had to do to survive, but that didn't make it any easier. I nodded my head to the others. They understood.

We tip-pawed over to Cruella and curled up next to her. Snuggling against the old bag of bones made us warm enough to fall asleep.

I saw Cruella's eyes flutter open. She saw us and glared. Then she smiled!

We all fell asleep.

* * *

I woke up to Roger's voice saying, "Cruella? What are you doing here?"

Dad and Roger had found the cave by following the sound of Cruella's snores. They'd seen the flare and had gone searching for whoever needed help.

"What am *I* doing here?" Cruella huffed. "Er . . . saving your dogs. You owe me."

Dad barked sternly. "Lucky! What are you doing here?"

"Er . . . surviving," I said. "We all worked together and survived the blizzard."

I gave my best smile. It was not a bad speech, I thought, but one look at Dad's face and I knew he wasn't buying it.

49

"You also disobeyed me," Dad barked. "When we get back to the farm, you're all grounded for a week."

"Aw, not that!" we begged. "Give us a break. That's cruel and unusual."

Dad stood firm. "You'll survive it—if you work together."

Chapter Eight

The Best Place in the World

 "I'm hungry," Rolly declared.

"Can't we go home yet?" Cadpig wondered. "Running away is going to make me miss all my shows."

I suddenly remembered that *Thunderbolt, P.I.* was on that night. I never miss *Thunderbolt*. Except for Dad, Thunderbolt's the bravest dog in the world!

Then I realized I wasn't being very brave

myself. "Um . . . maybe we should go home," I said.

Whatever had happened because of the disc, running away wouldn't solve it. Maybe there was some way I could make things up to Roger.

"It must be almost dinnertime by now," Rolly said.

"Okay," I agreed. "Let's go home!"

As soon as I'd made up my mind, I felt better. "Last one home is a rotten neighbor!" I barked as I took off at top speed.

Even the thought of Cruella didn't dampen my spirits. We were going home! And that's the greatest place in the world—even if it is next door to the worst neighbor.

When we got to the farm, Roger was in his office. The place was trashed even worse than Scorch and I had left it.

Roger stood in the middle of the mess, ripping apart the envelope that had held the disc. "Argh! Where is it?" he wailed.

My tail shot between my legs as I slunk into view.

"Lucky! Where have you been? I asked you to guard that disc with your life. How could you lose it?" Roger demanded.

My heart sank as I watched Roger pace back and forth. I'd

really blown it this time. I was beginning to wonder if I deserved a great home like the Dearly Farm.

It was no good blaming everything on my neighbor, Cruella. *I* was the one who'd disobeyed Roger, just as I'd been the one who decided to go camping, even though Dad said no. And the whole cone mess had really been my fault for smacking into Cruella at the picnic.

"Do you know what could happen if Cruella sees that game?" Roger fretted. "She'll screech right over here in that hideous car . . ."

Just then, I heard a horrible *screech*. Roger was too busy talking to notice.

He continued, ". . . she'll barge in through that door . . ."

I heard the door open with a loud *bang*, but Roger just kept ranting: ". . . and she'll shout . . ."

Cruella stood in the door- way. Her black-and-white hair swirled wildly around her head. Her beady eyes glared and her nostrils flared.

Then she gave a big grin and said, *"I love it!"*

Roger and I did the most amazing double take.

Cruella whipped out an endless scroll of paper and said, "Great game, Rodney. Now here are my notes."

* * *

I thought I would never stop laughing. I've got to say one thing for our neighbor, Cruella De Vil. With her living next door, there is never a dull moment . . . and that's okay with me!

Notes: